Akita

An Illustrated Story By
Freshawn Womack

Born on this day, are you, the Lotus Warrior, Akita.
You have not been fed in what feels like a millennium.
You hear the untamable cur within.
She needs to be made whole.
A canyon of darkness reaching out to claw at your back.
The hungry Tiger.
His bones ache.
Deprived of food.
His ribs visible from his frayed fur.
He no longer drools for a meal because he is dry and
dying.

Eyes meet like colliding
galaxies.
Destiny is the gravity
that propels you to act.
You must live on.
You must devour the
feral cat to become
stronger.
Eat.

You will last a bit longer, but you are not yet whole. He was the first of them who are parts of yourself. Sleep now, Akita, for your journey has only begun.

Akita, awaken!
He sniffs your face and greets you with a friendly kiss.
You are hungry, but this pup does not seem like something
you should eat. He is far too kind and makes you feel as if
you belong.
He walks with you as if he is your Acolyte.
Maybe you will find the next meal together.

Enter the forest of ivy, moss-covered trees, and budding flowers.

The Ram stands in the center, guarding the forest.

The forest is quiet, save the wind, howling at the leaves to churn, and his breathing. Loud, angered huffing.

He is the one you are searching for.

"You do not belong here," the Ram insists.

You are hungry. A belly filled with space. An
intimidating glare shakes you.
Your feet now of stone.
Heart of a hummingbird. Acolyte leaps forward.
He crouches low, resolve high and unwavering. You
are no longer afraid.

You make your stand.
Quicken. Rush. Clash.
He beckons you to leave. He is strong. You will
not leave until you are stronger. Toss and flip.
The Ram.
His stomach to the sun. Back to the earth.
Eat.

For a few seconds you can only hear Acolyte's and your
footsteps.
They come out one-by-one, then as if an avalanche.
The beasts of the forest come to celebrate your victory.
Too long had their "protector" kept out visitors and made
their air thick with tension. Now they are free.
You hear the forest singing with joy as you leave.
You cannot stay because this victory alone will not fill your
belly. You continue your journey.

You've been walking for days now.
Your feet feel like the sun that is beating down
on you. Your hunger burns brighter than the
flame in the sky. You worry about your pup, but
he is unscathed.
Is he smiling in reassurance or is that just how
he looks?
He stops because he smells it.
You do too.
Smoke of burning fowl.
You see nothing but cracked ground, dried
plants, and heat waves. Acolyte yips at the sun.
Something is approaching from it.

The Phoenix, powerful and brave, lands to meet you and Acolyte.
"No one intrudes on my domain," he says. "I am the strongest of this land and have claimed it as my own. Your presence incites a challenge!"
You're worried.
Acolyte lends you his sword to face your foe. From his golden beak rushes dazzling, crackling flames.
You fend them off with your blade.
You cut down the bird, only for him to rise anew, fresh with anger. Another attempt produces the same result.

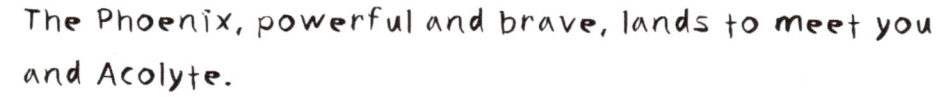

You are swallowed whole by the Phoenix. In his core is nothing but searing light. You should be afraid.
Yet you are calm.
Your breathing steady. Your core solid.
Your will is strong.
Eat.

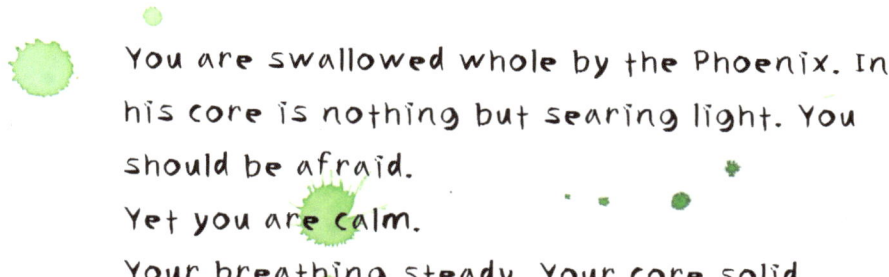

The bird is vanquished and you are stronger.
A cool breeze cradles you.
Upon leaving, you first see a sprout shoot up
from the ground.
You are now walking on a carpet of grass,
seeping up from the once dead ground. The soil
is fertile once again.
Onward you must go.
You are still hungry.

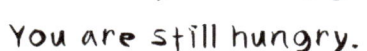

Rolling hills and gentle air.
The two of you rest your bodies, sitting
on one of the green mounds of earth.
Acolyte sleeps so soundly beside you.
His heart at ease amid each trouble faced.
You lay next to the pup.
You feel as if you knew him from
somewhere else.
He is familiar, though you met him only
days before.
You find yourself smiling.
You were alone for so long.
How long was it?
A soul that wanders.
Yet a feeling that stays.

You are being watched.
You stand, taking the sword you were given. A Shadow appears before you.
It points at the hole in its chest.
"I want!"
It jumps into Acolyte's body.
"I can feel!" the Shadow says.
It snarls at you, Akita. Acolyte is no longer in control. Foam from clenched teeth.
Hairs wild, as if charged by static. You cannot hurt him.
He is not himself.

"Now I keep," says the Shadow. He
lunges forward.
Extended claws.
He is stopped.
Caught by your embrace.
Warm heart melting the cold darkness.
Eat.
Acolyte is free. So is your heart.

The sky is darkened.

Air moistened by this rain wreaks of sadness.

You are on a trail, furnished with solemn trees.

A mountain peaks out above the trees at the end of
the trail.

Acolyte stops, barking at something rustling in the
leaves bushes. You feel a presence and ready your
sword.

A shrouded woman creeps onto the path.

She inches closer. Close enough to see her pale,
somber face.

It is hard to tell if those are tears or the rain.

Her eyes are worn and needing something you can
give. She points to your sword, Akita.

Then to herself.

You shake your head, taken aback. Confused.

A howling screech bellows from her throat. It seems to pierce your hand-covered ears and straight into your soul. The Banshee doubles over, spitting out syrupy, cerulean blood.

She looks to you.

She is tired.

You understand.

Her message clear.

Eat.

"I'm sorry," you softly say.

The rain lightens, but you know the hardest part has yet to come. The mountain is ahead.

You have made it to the summit.
This fog makes you unable to see the ground.
You walk through the clouds, nervously eyeing anything
that moves. There should be the sounds of wind, but only
a deafening silence persists. Acolyte is close to you.
He looks to you. He knows you have nothing to fear.
You brush his head with your hand.
Finally, you hear breathing. Low. From every direction.
You are unsure of the source.
Reaching for your sword.
"There will be no need for that," says the thundering
voice.
"Who are you?" you ask.
The beast materializes from the mist.

3.

3 eyes.

3 heads.

Cerberus is blocking the gate to the other side.

"I'm glad to see you here again," he says. " This time, you are
stronger."

"I do not understand," is your reply.

"You have been here before, Akita," he begins. "Think of yourself as a
dream. When a one occurs, it can be vivid. One may be unaware it is a
dream. And you are a recurring dream."

"I am the dream, but who is the dreamer?"

"Ah. Only the sleeper knows."

"If I am a dream, I hope I am a pleasant one."

"Worry not. Recurring dreams mean there is something to be
understood."

"What do I need to know?" you ask.

"Yourself."

You look to Acolyte. You knew him before as other dreams
you have been.
Time lost and everything gained.
"You seem to have an inkling," Cerberus says.
"I believe so."
"Then you know what is next?"
"Yes," you reply. "It is time for me to awaken."

Eat.

The gate shines from the opening. You
approach.
Acolyte barks at you. You'll miss his smile.
You embrace him.
"Thank you for being by my side, giving me
strength and courage." You enter the gate.

Shiva sits alone in the temperate, flowery meadow. "Come," he says.

You join him.

"Are you afraid?"

"I am not," you say.

"Why is that?"

"I see now that I am a reiteration of my past and future selves."

"What about beyond that," Shiva asks. "You are not separate from the very structure of the cosmos. A body dies and is reconfigured as another living being or object. The Great All is one organism, recycling its many, complex and beautiful parts. So what are you?"

You ponder this thought.

"I am a function of the universe. One of many that progress it forward."

"Do you you wish to fight it?" he asks.

"No," you say, putting down your sword.

There is only
darkness.
Not cold.
Not heat.
Not anything.
All the colors come
together.

Even from the darkness, stars shine.
A dream.
A nova.
A dog that sleeps.
He awakens.
His dream forgotten.
He feels wiser, stronger, and whole.
Whatever it was, his dream made him feel at peace.
A thought that wanders.
A feeling that stays.
A dream to further the soul.
Though fleeting, it can be strong enough to progress the understanding of one's own place in the universe.
Dream until she is realized.

Eat.